THREE
BOYS
TALK
BALL

Three Boys Talk Ball
Copyright © 2023 by Ted Dorff

Published in the United States of America

ISBN Paperback: 978-1-960629-75-3
ISBN Hardback: 979-8-89091-067-7
ISBN eBook: 978-1-960629-76-0

All rights reserved. No part of this publication may be reproduced, stored in a retrieval system or transmitted in any way by any means, electronic, mechanical, photocopy, recording or otherwise without the prior permission of the author except as provided by USA copyright law.

The opinions expressed by the author are not necessarily those of ReadersMagnet, LLC.

ReadersMagnet, LLC
10620 Treena Street, Suite 230 | San Diego, California, 92131 USA
1.619. 354. 2643 | www.readersmagnet.com

Book design copyright © 2023 by ReadersMagnet, LLC. All rights reserved.

Cover design by Ericka Obando
Interior design by Daniel Lopez
Illustrated by Yoshie Kudo Dorff

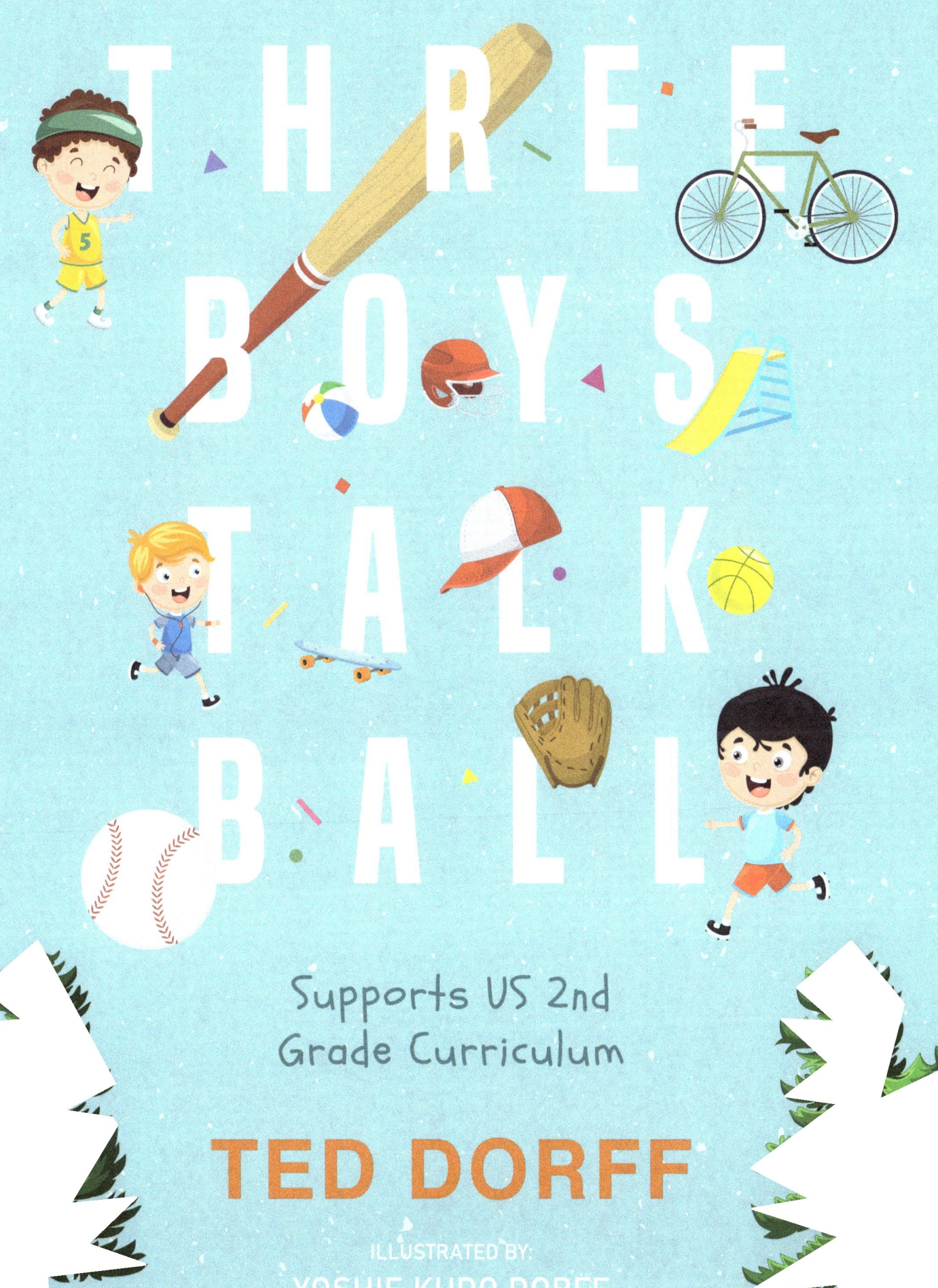

THREE BOYS TALK BALL

Supports US 2nd Grade Curriculum

TED DORFF

ILLUSTRATED BY:
YOSHIE KUDO DORFF

Jim, Jimmer, and James are neighbors.

They play together on the street, in their yards, and at school.

They are inseparable, but they have one interesting difference, which is in how they talk about things.

Jim is nice, but speaks very little, and doesn't describe things much. He likes the facts, just the facts. He says as little as possible. He uses very few colorful words describing what he says.

Jimmer, on the other hand, always has an adjective or two to give color and life to everything he talks about. Somehow he has learned to see and describe details. It helps people understand his stories and not get bored. People take interest when he talks and can see in their mind the scenes he describes. Sometimes he compares things he is talking about to other things in order to help people understand. That seems to make things "come alive!" He also asks questions that make others think.

Then there is James. He describes everything as if he is not involved, kind of like an observer. He talks about things in a way that you would almost wonder if he was there or just quoting someone else. He isn't a zombie and definitely has a personality, but when he talks, it is about other people and things as if he isn't in the action. It's as if he were up in the air looking down on things. Some call that "passive voice." He also is often the last one to speak in a conversation with some kind of statement that leaves everyone speechless. He usually has the last word, just because Jim and Jimmer don't know what to say after James makes a conversation-ending statement. Most of their conversations have started with Jim. Jimmer embellished it. Then James would have the last word.

One time when the boys were walking home after school, they saw a dog that had gotten away from his owner. The owner was a frantic lady running down the street toward the boys. When she asked them if they had seen the dog, James' way of speaking was just what she needed.

James told her, "A waist-high brown dog was seen dragging his leash running past us 30 seconds ago. He then turned the next corner to the right."
"Thank you so much!" the lady said as she rushed past them.

There is nothing wrong with their different styles of communication. In fact, usually they are really tight. They get along great. If Jim starts a topic, Jimmer will surely make it interesting and engaging. James might add some interesting facts the others might not know. Without hearing the tone of his voice, it would be hard to know how he feels when he talks. When they play, none of that matters much. They're still buddies. Whatever they are playing, they enjoy each other, but they all love to play games that involve balls, which makes it that much more fun!

Let's look at their time together and see how they describe the same thing differently.

As the three left their houses one morning, Jim said,
"Good morning! Happy Monday!"

Jimmer replied, "Good morning. What a bright day with flowers! There are so many birds out that I wish I could fly around with them. I wonder if the birds have different songs for different occasions. What do you think?"

James concluded, "It's the first Monday of spring. The morning is the same for everyone. There's no way to know what a bird's song means."

As they walked to school, Jim said, "Watch out for that car!"

Jimmer said, "That's one ruby red car! It's going faster than a roadrunner and the tires are screeching dangerously around the corner because he really should slow down! Would you drive like a maniac when you get older?"

James concluded, "The car was a danger to everyone on the road and should slow down."

Jim remembered, "We have a baseball game after school."

"I can't wait! I love to dart after balls in the outfield like the way my dog chases after rabbits and squirrels when we hike trails. Sometimes when batters hit long fly balls, I try to jump as high as I can to catch them before they go over my head! Except that girl Jamie always hits them beyond my reach. I think she plays better than all of us!" Jimmer added.

"Most batters can't hit balls over the heads of the outfielders. By the way, Jim, thank you for reminding me about the game. I'm so hungry I almost forgot!" James completed.

"When I go to watch professional games with my dad,
I try to catch home runs and foul balls." Jim said.

Jimmer said, "Me too. I yell at the top of my lungs until my throat tingles and my dad's forehead gets wrinkled because of the creative heckling I give to the other team's batters.
I call for outfielders to throw foul balls to me.

I keep one hand in my glove at all times so I'm ready.
I'm so excited when a ball comes anywhere close that if I had a tail,
it would be wagging so hard it would be hitting people on both sides of me!"

"It's important to have a glove when people sit in the stands and to watch where the ball is at all times," James said. "I heard Jamie caught a ball at a professional game once. One has to not only be good, but lucky to catch a ball at a professional game. She is lucky *and* good."

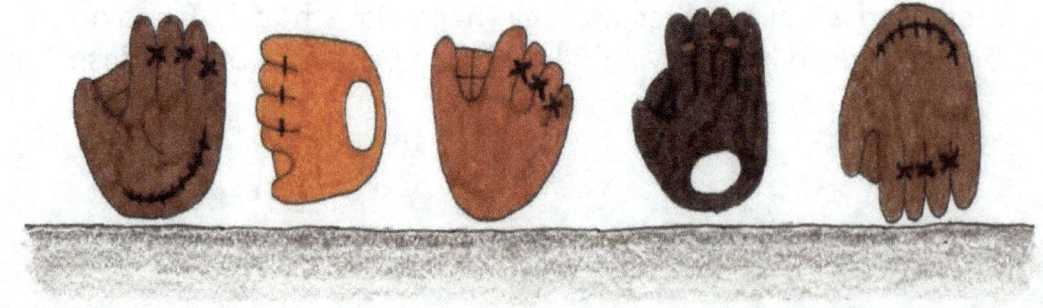

Jim continued, "I love stadium hot dogs!"

Jimmer added, "I love the sweet and sour relish they have and spicy mustard. I squirt the tangy ketchup at the stadium all over my hot dog and pile grilled onions on top! My dad taught me to eat grilled onions. At first I didn't like them, but now I love them! I ask for "the works" and love the feeling of all those flavors in my stomach! My mom says I'm going to get sick one day if I keep doing that and that will make me hate hot dogs. She's right about a lot of things, but I never, ever get sick of them!"

Then James stated, "Hot dogs aren't liked by everyone and my mom says they're bad for everyone."

"After the game I'm so tired." Jim said.

"I'm like a helpless jellyfish on the soft car seat by the time we get home. My dad carries me like a rag doll to my bed." replied Jimmer.
"Often sleeping kids get carried by parents to their beds, but they don't realize it until the next morning." James said.

"Someday I want to be a professional baseball player." Jim said.

"Me too!" Jimmer began. "I dream of taking a humble, confident bow from a spit-filled pitcher's mound at a packed stadium full of admiring fans chanting my very own name. Jimmer! Jimmer! JA-AMES!! Actually, wouldn't it be great if all of us got to be pros? I'll bet Jamie will be a pro. That girl has power!"

"Only home crowds shout names nicely." James said.

"Jimmer, you have a way with words!" Jim said to Jimmer.
"Jimmer really does talk about things so much that
I can see them in my mind." James concluded.

Jimmer threw his arms over his pals, "I just think there are so many cool things happening all of the time. Well, you are the best friends a little dreamer could ever hope to have! Either way, I'm sure your dreams of the future are just as vivid as mine! I admit that my mom is right, though; she says that sometimes I should talk in a way that is to the point, short and sweet or just give the facts."

"Maybe. Enough talking! All I know is
I feel like playing some ball now!" said Jim.

"C'mon! Let's go! Some ball needs to be thrown and caught." said James. Off the three boys went to play ball together...and of course, they kept talking as they went, each in their own special way.

This book helps teach concepts from the 2nd grade public curriculum, regarding communication styles, adjectives, and descriptive language.

. . .

About the author: **Ted Dorff** is from California, but lives in New Mexico. Ted is known as a resourceful dreamer. He has submitted dozens of ideas for patents, one of which is used in nearly every smartphone ever made, but most of them have remained in his personal notes. Having worked for several of the most influential high tech companies in the world, he considers himself a minimalist and a homebody. A father of one daughter, he has volunteered extensively with children and youth groups for decades.

. . .

About the illustrator: **Yoshie Kudo Dorff** was born in Sapporo, Hokkaido, Japan. She moved to the USA in 1986. She has lived in California, Washington, Massachusetts, Pennsylvania, and Utah. Yoshie gained notoriety for her pen drawings and writing, among other creative hobbies such as quilting. Her favorite pastime is spending time with her grandchildren.

10620 Treena Street, Suite 230
San Diego, California,
CA 92131 USA
www.readersmagnet.com
1.619.354.2643
Copyright 2023 All Rights Reserved